MADELINE
AT THE WHITE HOUSE

Story and pictures by
John Bemelmans Marciano

VIKING
An Imprint of Penguin Group (USA) Inc.

For Galatea

VIKING
Published by Penguin Group
Penguin Young Readers Group, 345 Hudson Street, New York, New York 10014, U.S.A.
Penguin Group (Canada), 90 Eglinton Avenue East, Suite 700, Toronto, Ontario, Canada M4P 2Y3
(a division of Pearson Penguin Canada Inc.)
Penguin Books Ltd, 80 Strand, London WC2R 0RL, England
Penguin Ireland, 25 St Stephen's Green, Dublin 2, Ireland (a division of Penguin Books Ltd)
Penguin Group (Australia), 250 Camberwell Road, Camberwell, Victoria 3124, Australia
(a division of Pearson Australia Group Pty Ltd)
Penguin Books India Pvt Ltd, 11 Community Centre, Panchsheel Park, New Delhi – 110 017, India
Penguin Group (NZ), 67 Apollo Drive, Rosedale, North Shore 0632, New Zealand (a division of Pearson New Zealand Ltd.)
Penguin Books (South Africa) (Pty) Ltd, 24 Sturdee Avenue, Rosebank, Johannesburg 2196, South Africa

Penguin Books Ltd, Registered Offices: 80 Strand, London WC2R 0RL, England

ISBN: 978-0-670-01228-2

Printed at RR Donnelley Reynosa, Tamaulipas, Mexico December 2010
Set in Bodoni

In an old white house in Washington, D.C.,

Lived as lonely a girl as there can be.
Her name was Miss Penelope Randall,
But everyone always called her Candle
On account of a wildly stubborn curl
That like a flame would dance and twirl.

She needed an appointment to see her father.
But he always canceled so why did she bother?

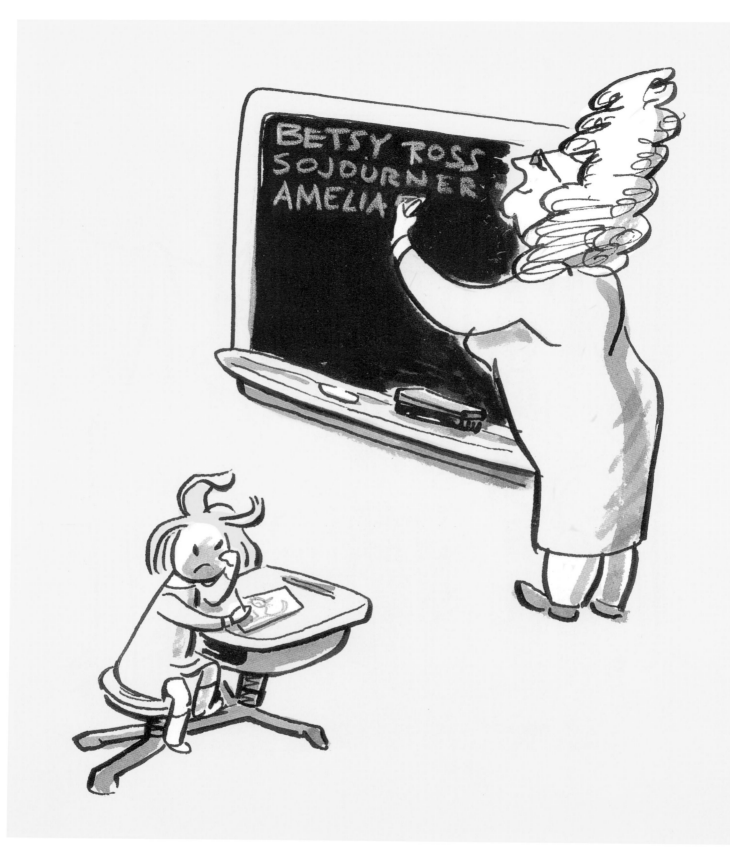

She sat bored and alone at her desk and stool,
The only student of the White House school.

Secret Service Agent Downs

Made sure she never left the grounds.

But life took a turn for the better
When from her mother came a letter.
It read:

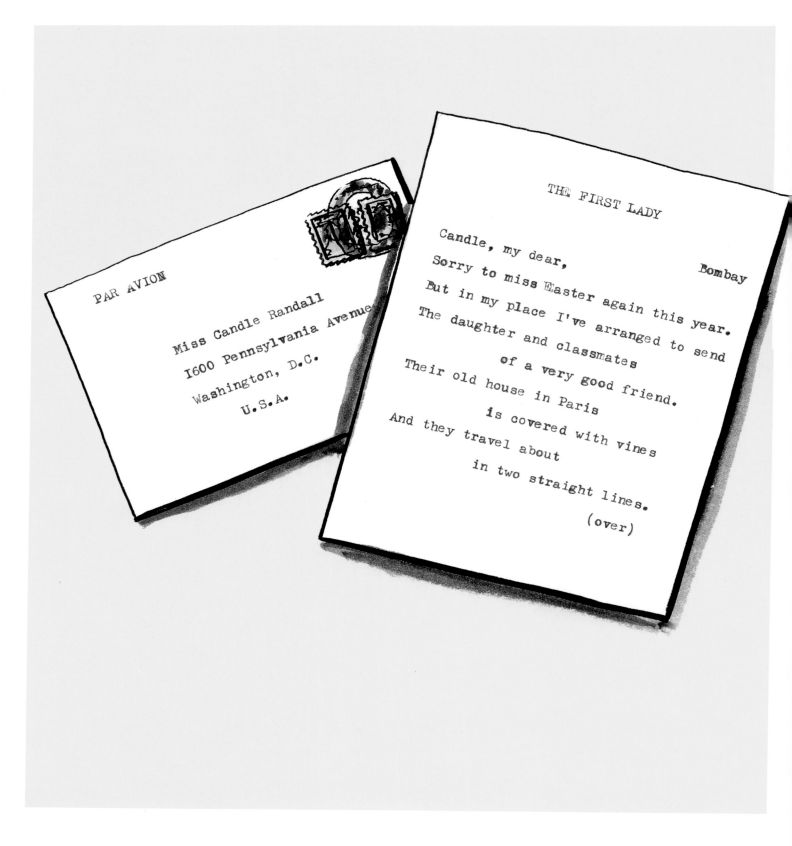

PAR AVION

Miss Candle Randall
1600 Pennsylvania Avenue
Washington, D.C.
U.S.A.

THE FIRST LADY

Candle, my dear,   Bombay
Sorry to miss Easter again this year.
But in my place I've arranged to send
The daughter and classmates
         of a very good friend.
Their old house in Paris
         is covered with vines
And they travel about
         in two straight lines.
                    (over)

Their plane gets in at half past nine.

The smallest one is Madeline.

Eleven girls were very shy,
But Madeline looked her straight in the eye
And said to Candle, "How do you do?
It's very nice to be meeting you."

The girls were taken to their quarters.
"Time to unpack," were Miss Clavel's orders.

Madeline's bag contained a SURPRISE!

A rabbit! Or rather, a friend in disguise.

Madeline's magician had stowed away
To join them for the holiday.
The girls all cried "Hip hip HOORAY!"

And went to Candle's room to play.

The girls bid good night to their new friend.

Candle was sad that it had to end.

She went to bed without delay.

She could hardly wait for the following day.

The White House Easter celebration

Is the most fun festival in the nation!

They hunted Easter eggs at noon,

And then they rolled them with a spoon.

Ice cream, pie, and chocolate cake

Can lead to quite a tummyache.

Madeline asked, "Would it be all right
If I stayed in Candle's room tonight?"
Miss Clavel weakly nodded yes.
(Her stomach too was in distress.)
"Just go to sleep early—that's a warning!
Our plane leaves first thing in the morning."

They played dress-up,

Cards,

And had a lark,

And told scary stories in the dark.

But when the cuckoo sang the hour
The frolicking mood turned quickly sour.
The night—where could it have gone?
All too soon would come the dawn.
Madeline would soon be leaving—
Oh, how Candle started grieving!

The poor girl cried, "Boohoo!
Why can't I fly away too?
Outside my window the world looks pretty
But I've never even seen the city."

The rabbit took this as his cue—
A magician knows just what to do.
He raised his arms like a candelabra
And chanted the word "ABRACADABRA!"

The rabbit conjured something awesome:
A magic tide of cherry blossom!

Had two girls ever flown so high

Up into the starry sky?

The rising sun erased the moon.
Miss Clavel would wake up soon.

But on and on they tempted fate.
They were almost home . . .

Perhaps too late!
From the hall outside, Miss Clavel knocked
And tried the door, but it was locked.
"Are you there, Madeline? We're in a hurry!"
Said Miss Clavel, quite sick with worry.

Agent Downs, a good bit bolder,
Broke the door open with his shoulder.

The girls, they saw, were fast asleep.
But there was a schedule to keep.

Miss Clavel said, "Madeline, make haste,
We haven't any time to waste."

To say good-bye is always sad,

But coming home is never bad.

Miss Clavel came in that night
And checked the girls by candlelight.
To all the beds she walked around
To see the girls were safe and sound.
Then with a smile, she closed the door.
That's all there is, there isn't any more.

A background note to MADELINE AT THE WHITE HOUSE

The idea for sending Madeline to the White House was my grandfather's and grew out of his friendship with Jacqueline Kennedy. In a series of letters from late 1961 and early 1962, my grandfather sounded out the First Lady on ideas for the book, which he proposed calling "Madeline Visits Caroline," with text by Mrs. Kennedy herself. At the time, he was still working on "Madeline and the Magician," an expanded version of "Madeline's Christmas." In this book the Magician, named Mustapha, was sent away by Miss Clavel, but returned at the end in the form of a lonely meowing cat wearing a fez, a ruse that would allow him to stay with the girls forever.

My grandfather died in 1962, before the Magician book was finished or the White House one even begun. A proud veteran of the First World War, he was buried in Arlington Cemetery, which you will find on the endpapers of this book. Although French was his first language and he grew up largely in Germany, my grandfather immigrated to New York as a teenager and considered himself first and foremost a proud American.

One of my favorite pictures of my grandfather's is the sketch for the final page of "Madeline and the Magician," in which Mustapha the cat is surrounded by the girls. I imagine that it is actually my grandfather who is the magician, and certainly it is Madeline and the girls with whom he will stay forever.

J.B.M.

Places visited in the book:

At the White House

Oval Office

Lincoln Bedroom

South Lawn

On the Magic Ride

Lincoln Memorial

Dome of the Capitol

Jefferson Memorial

Washington Monument

On the Endpapers

Arlington National Cemetery

THE TOMB OF THE